Meesh the BAD DEMON

MICHELLE LAM

WITH COLORS BY LAUREN "PERRY" WHEELER

ALFRED A. KNOPF  NEW YORK

THIS IS A BORZOI BOOK PUBLISHED BY ALFRED A. KNOPF

Visit us on the Web! rhcbooks.com

Educators and librarians, for a variety of teaching tools, visit us at RHTeachersLibrarians.com

Library of Congress Cataloging-in-Publication Data is available upon request.
ISBN 978-0-593-37287-6 (trade) — ISBN 978-0-593-37288-3 (lib. bdg.) —
ISBN 978-0-593-37289-0 (ebook) — ISBN 978-0-593-37286-9 (trade pbk.)

The text of this book is set in Caffe Lungo.
The illustrations were created using Photoshop.
Book design by Michelle Cunningham
With colors by Lauren "Perry" Wheeler

MANUFACTURED IN CHINA
10 9 8 7 6 5 4 3 2 1

First Edition

To my grandparents, Chow Yee Cheung,
Lai Cheung, Tsang Lam, and Yeung Ng Lam,
and my parents, Caren Cheung and Kenneth Lam,
for dealing with the REAL Meesh growing up.

MOUNT MAGMA
MOUNT MAGMA
HOME OF THE DEMONS, LAND OF THE LAVA
EACH NIGHT, DEMONS WORK UNTIL SUNRISE, PURIFYING THEIR LAVA.
CRNNKK

WITHOUT LAVA, THERE IS NO LIFE IN MOUNT MAGMA.
WORKING AT A LAVA PLANT . . .
IS THE FATE OF ALMOST EVERY DEMON.

GOOD JOB TODAY, CHOW!
SURE THING! CATCH YOU KIDS LATER!

OH, MEESH?

GRANDMA!
YOU'RE BACK JUST IN TIME!
BROUGHT YOU SOME
BUB-LAVA BACK FROM WORK.
YES!
THAT'S PERFECT
FOR DINNER!

OH, IS IT ALREADY THE *PRINCESS NOUNA* FINALE?
YEAH! IT'S GOING TO BE EPIC!

HAHA, I'M SURE IT WILL BE.

MAYBE WE CAN WATCH *THE LOST STORY OF MOUNT MAGMA* AS OUR NEXT SHOW?
WHAT? THAT SOUNDS SO BORING!

WHY WATCH THAT WHEN WE CAN SEE FAIRIES FIGHT CRIME?!
IF WE'RE GONNA GO VISIT PLUMERIA CITY SOMEDAY, WE GOTTA KNOW EVERYTHING ABOUT FAIRIES NOW!

OK. OK.

MAYBE YOU'LL ENJOY HISTORY MORE WHEN YOU'RE OLDER. . . .

OH, MIGHTY RUBY, SHINE BRIGHT!

DESTROY THIS EVIL WITH ALL YOUR LIGHT!

THAT WAS—
AMAZING!!!

I HATE TO BE A PARTY POOPER, BUT GUESS WHAT TIME IT IS?

YOU DON'T HAVE TO TELL ME!
OH, I KNOW. YOU'RE STILL MY LITTLE DEMON NO MATTER WHAT.

IT'S LITTLE FAIRY!
DREAM

OH! WELL, REST UP THIS MORNING, FAIRY MEESH!

LOVE YOU,
GRANDMA!
GOOD
MORNING!
PLOP!
DREAM

DREAM

10:00

14:00
Beep
beep
18:10

DREAM
DREAM
GASP!

YOU CAN HAVE MY BREAKFAST—I GOTTA GO!
SO EARLY?!

HUFF
HUFF
HUFF

MOUNT MAGMA MIDDLE SCHOOL

HEY, OLIVIA, SORRY I'M LATE.
AHA!

SO THIS IS WHERE YOU'VE BEEN.

WAIT, XAVIER—

MOVE, PINKY.

YOU'RE SKIPPING CLASS FOR
A FLOWER?!
YOU KNOW THAT'S . . .
NO!
NOT ALLOWED.
RIPPP!!!
RRRR

MAYBE YOU SHOULD ACTUALLY GO TO CLASS FOR ONCE.

AND STOP TALKING TO PLANTS OR SOMETHING.

AND THAT, CLASS, IS HOW YOU BREATHE FIRE.

HOLD 2 SEC.

BREATHE WITH YOUR BELLY

OH, HELLO, MEESH. YOU'RE LATE. **AGAIN.**

ALL BECAUSE OF A FLOWER, I HEARD?

UH . . .

WELL, THEN . . .

YOU CLEARLY HAD TIME TO PRACTICE FIRE BREATHING, RIGHT?

SO, WHY DON'T YOU SHOW ALL OF US?
B- BUT—

DON'T BE SHY!

. . .

AHEM . . .

BWEH!

HA
HA
HA
HA
HA
HA

HA
HA
HA
MAYBE YOU'LL GET IT NEXT TIME— WHEN YOU'RE NOT LATE.
NICE ONE, PINKY.
PFT
XAVIER, WHY DON'T YOU SHOW THE CLASS HOW IT'S DONE?
YES!!!
BREATHE WITH YOUR BELLY

WOW! HOW ARE YOU SO GOOD?!
OH, YOU KNOW, I ACTUALLY PRACTICE INSTEAD OF PICKING FLOWERS!
ALL RIGHT, SEE YOU NEXT CLASS!

ACID-PUKING CLASS
OK, STUDENTS, YOU'LL REALLY WANT TO UTILIZE YOUR GAG REFLEX WITH THIS ONE.
YOUR STOMACH ACID CAN BE USED AS A DEFENSE DURING AN EMERGENCY.
SO TRY TO THINK OF SOMETHING DISGUSTING. IT COULD BE SUNSHINE, RAINBOWS, OR UNICORNS. . . .
WAIT, WHAT?

HORN-SHARPENING CLASS
UGH, NOT AGAIN.
PFT.

NIGHT VISION CLASS
YOU'RE SUPPOSED TO SEE IN THE DARK, NOT GLOW IN THE DARK!
AH!

LAVA-MOLDING CLASS
IT BURNS!

LATER . . .

NO *PRINCESS NOUNA* RERUNS TONIGHT?

MEESH?

LET ME GUESS . . .
IT'S THE KIDS AT SCHOOL AGAIN?
THEY MADE FUN OF ME TALKING TO A FLOWER.

OH, MEESH, THOSE KIDS JUST DON'T HAVE AS BIG OF AN IMAGINATION AS YOU!

NOT EVERY DEMON HAS TO BE LIKE THE KIDS AT—

IT'S OK. I DON'T WANT TO BE LIKE THEM ANYWAY.

OH.

YOU KNOW . . .

THERE ARE TIMES I FEEL LIKE I DON'T BELONG, EITHER.
HUH?
B-BUT WHY?! YOU'RE, LIKE, THE COOLEST GRANDMA IN MOUNT MAGMA!
HA! THAT'S JUST HOW IT SEEMS . . .
WHEN I FIRST STARTED WORKING AT THE LAVA TREATMENT PLANT, I WAS THE OLDEST ONE.
YOU SURE YOU GOT THAT?
YEP.
CAREFUL THERE.

I WAS THE OLDEST FEMALE, TOO, OF COURSE.
HEY, GRANNY! ARE YOU CRAZY?!
YOU KIDS NEED TO RELAX.
THAT'S A BOILING BUCKET OF FRESH LAVA!
IT TOOK A WHILE FOR THE OTHERS TO TRULY BELIEVE IN ME.
AND EVEN THOUGH THEY ACCEPT ME NOW, I KNOW THAT . . .
I'M STILL NEVER GOING TO FIT IN.

AND I'M OK WITH THAT BECAUSE . . .
IT MEANS I GET TO DRINK BUB-LAVA AND WATCH *PRINCESS NOUNA* WITH MY MEESH!
SORRY, GRANDMA. I NEVER KNEW YOU FELT THAT WAY.
HEY, BEING DIFFERENT REALLY ISN'T AS BAD AS YOU THINK.

IN FACT, I ACTUALLY LIKE BEING UNIQUE. MAYBE SOMEDAY YOU'LL FEEL THAT WAY, TOO.

YOU'RE NOT A BAD DEMON JUST BECAUSE YOU LIKE FLOWERS AND FAIRIES, OKAY?
YEAH . . . I GUESS.

. . .

IT'S OK TO FEEL BAD, BUT DON'T SULK FOR TOO LONG.

IF THEY BULLY YOU AGAIN, YOU HAVE MY PERMISSION TO BEAT THEM UP.

KIDDING! DON'T DO THAT. ANYWAY, GOOD MORNING!

SIGH.

WHY CAN'T I JUST BE LIKE PRINCESS NOUNA, LIVING IN PLUMERIA CITY . . . ?

THE NEXT NIGHT . . .

NOW DON'T ACTUALLY BEAT THOSE KIDS UP, OK?
HAHA, I WON'T!

SEE YOU LATER!

I'LL RACE YA TO SCHOOL!

HEY! THAT'S CHEATING!

HAHA, BLECH!
GRR.

UGH, DEMON BOYS ARE THE WORST.

LEMME SHOW YOU WHAT I DID FOR OUR PROJECT SO FAR!

I MADE A LOT OF PROGRESS WITH THE INTRO.
AHH!

STEP BACK!
AGAIN?!
NO!
STEP FORWARD!
I GOT IT! I GOT IT!

OH, THANKS! YOU'RE MEESH FROM THE OTHER CLASS, RIGHT?
WE HEARD ABOUT YOUR FIRE BREATHING!

AW, SO CUTE!

S-SORRY!

WHOOPS.

EXCUSE ME, ONLY CUSTOMERS ARE ALLOWED BEYOND THIS POINT.

GROSS.

LAVA ACCIDENT?
SPICE
SNAILGARDEN

LATE AGAIN?!

YOU KNOW MS. ROWSH SENT ME OUT TO LOOK FOR YOU AGAIN, RIGHT?!
SO WHAT? I DON'T HAVE ANY MORE FLOWERS FOR YOU TO KILL.
I HOPE YOU KNOW YOU'RE GONNA FAIL AT THIS POINT!
ALL OF US WORK HARD. MEANWHILE, YOU'RE . . .
HUH?

WHAT'S THIS?

A FAIRY TOY?

GIVE THAT BACK!

HEY, XAVIER, WHAT'S TAKING SO LONG?

WOW . . .
YOU'RE SUCH A DISGRACE TO DEMONS.
I AM NOT A DEMON!

HEY, STOP!
DON'T TOUCH MY STUFF!
AGH!
GET OFF OF ME!
YOU STARTED THIS!
XAVIER! MEESH!
STOP! YOU'LL ROLL OFF THE CLIFF!
HEY!
I SAID GET OFF!

AHHHHHHHH!!!!

NO!

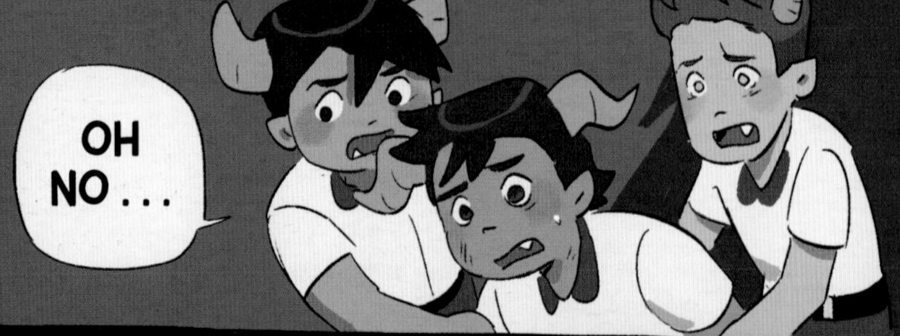

OH NO . . .

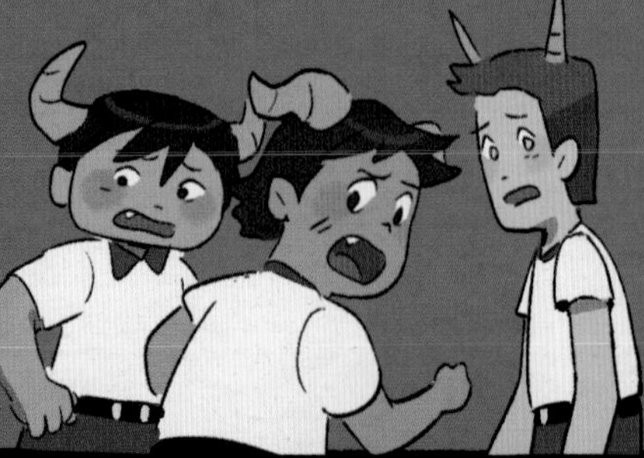

WE HAVE TO GO GET HELP!

OOF!
AH!
HNG!
UGH . . .

UGH . . .

WHAT TIME IS IT?
UGH, XAVIER . . .
WAIT!
PHEW . . .
SHE'S OK.

MOM, MOM! LOOK!
HEY, JUST LEAVE IT ALONE. WE HAVE NICER TOYS AT HOME.
BUT IT GLOWS!
SEE? LOOK! MY ROBOTS DON'T EVEN GLOW LIKE THIS!

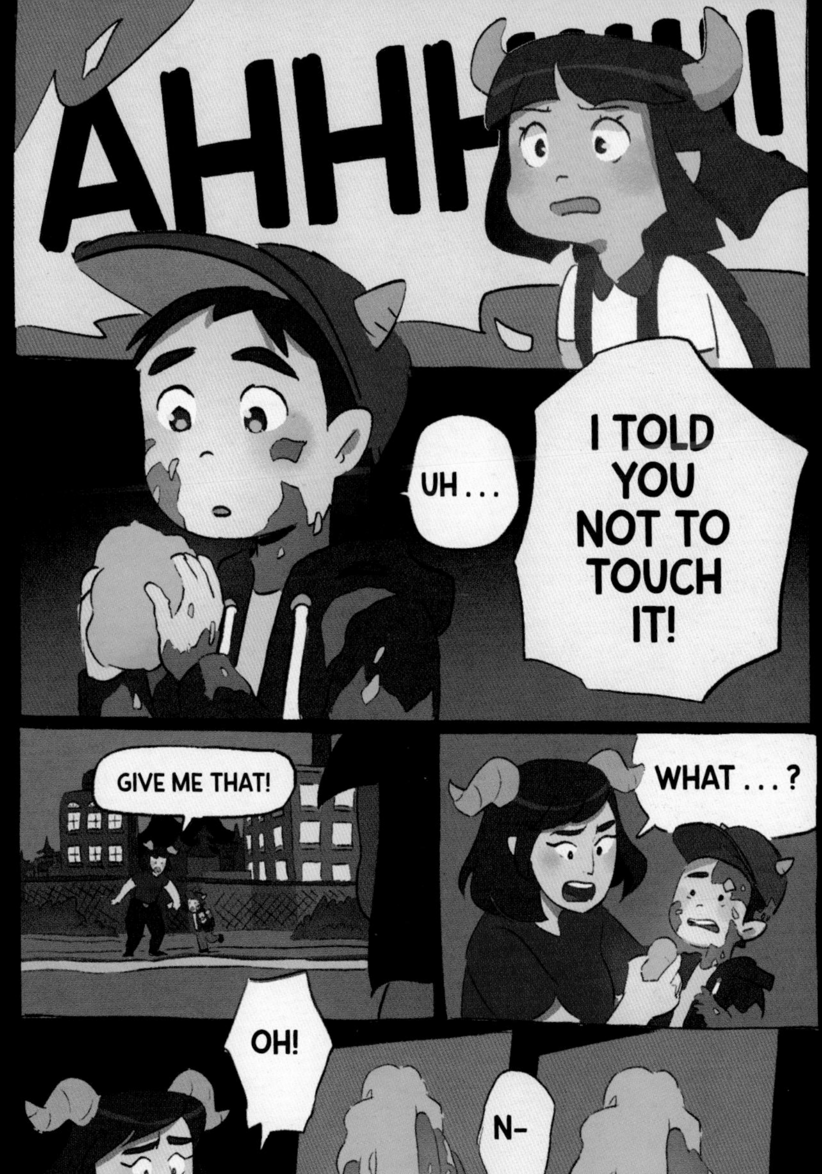
AHHHHHH!
UH...
I TOLD YOU NOT TO TOUCH IT!
GIVE ME THAT!
WHAT...?
OH!
N-
NO!

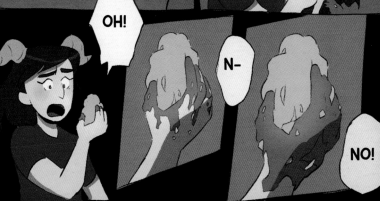

AHHHHH!!
STOP!
AHH!
HELP!!!!

HELP!
HELP!
SOMEONE JUST TURNED TO STONE!
DON'T TOUCH THE GREEN STUFF!
HUH?
HEY, KID, YOU OK?
THE GREEN STUFF WILL TURN YOU TO STONE!
UH, WHAT? SHOULDN'T YOU BE IN SCHOOL?
A LITTLE DIRT NEVER HURT ANYONE.
UH . . .

BEHIND YOU!
WHAT IS THAT?!
AH!
UH . . . GUYS?
I FEEL KINDA . . .
OH NO!
AHHH!!!

WHAT IS HAPPENING?!
DON'T TOUCH IT!
WHY NOT?!
RUN!!!

GRANDMA!
GRANDMA?!
M-MEESH?

GRANDMA! WE HAVE TO GET OUT OF HERE!
COME ON!
NO, MEESH! DON'T GET ANY CLOSER!
I'M NOT LEAVING WITHOUT YOU!
THE LAVA IS POISONED!
IF YOU DON'T GO NOW, IT'LL GET YOU, TOO!
GO FIND HELP!
SAVE US.

LIKE PRINCESS NOUNA WOULD.
G-GRANDMA?

HUH?
WHAT'S THIS?
IT'S COMING. . . .
I LOVE YOU.

THE RUBY HEALS ALL!
THE RUBY!

HUFF
HUFF

CRCK

WOOOOOSH
UH...
HELLO?

WAAAH . . .

AH!

WAAAH . . .
WAAAH . . .
HUH?

ARE YOU . . .
CRYING?

WAAAH...
WAAAH...

YOU'RE ALL SAD?

WAAAH...

OH, SORRY FOR BEING SCARED.

I GUESS I'M...
ALSO SAD.

PAT PAT
PAT

HEH. THANKS.

AH!

HA HA
HA HA HA
OH!

LOOK! I'M FLYING!

A DEMON? THAT FLIES? ISN'T THAT WILD!

I HAVE TO SAY, PLANTS ARE THE BEST LISTENERS!

I FEEL A BIT BETTER, TOO. . . .

HUH?

THE NECKLACE?

THAT'S WEIRD. . . .

GRANDMA . . .
OH, I'M TRYING TO FIND PLUMERIA CITY.
. . .
DO YOU KNOW WHERE THAT IS?
. . . ?
WHOA!

NO WAY...
AH!
WOOO!

THANK YOU, TREES!
WOW!
CLOUD JUMPING?! JUST LIKE IN *PRINCESS NOUNA*!

HA!
WOO!
MFFF!
WHOA!
AHHH!

AHHHHH!!

I—I'M HERE?!

HEY!
EXCUSE ME! CAN YOU LET ME IN?

STOP RIGHT THERE.

DO YOU HAVE A TICKET FOR ENTRY?
UH . . . NO?

WELL, THEN, I'M AFRAID I CAN'T LET YOU IN.
WHAT?! WHY NOT?!
IN CASE YOU WEREN'T AWARE . . .
THE CITY IS HOSTING A SPECIAL EVENT TODAY . . .
AND WE CAN'T JUST LET *ANYONE* IN.
SORRY, MAYBE NEXT TIME.

WHAT IF THERE IS NO NEXT TIME?
HMM . . .
ROSES?
SNIFF
AH—
AH-CHOO!
WHOA . . .

AHA!
THAT GUY DOESN'T KNOW HE'S DEALING WITH A DEMON!
IT'S GLOWING AGAIN?
FARMERS' MARKET

HEY!

C'MON!
HURRY!
IF WE GET THERE EARLY, WE CAN GET A SELFIE WITH PRINCESS NOUNA!

ADOPT A
PUP TODAY
FAIRY'S BREATH
Cherry Lips
PUP TODAY!
FAIRY'S BREATH
I'M ACTUALLY HERE.
I CAN'T BELIEVE IT. . . .

IT'S JUST LIKE THE TV SHOW.

!

PRETTY . . .

OH, RIGHT . . .

STAY FOCUSED!

IT'S THE REAL THING.
FATIMA?
YES, THAT'S ME.
YOU MAY ENTER.

ARE YOU EXCITED TO SEE PRINCESS NOUNA?

YOU'D BETTER BE!

YEAH!

YOUR OUTFIT'S SUPER CUTE, BY THE WAY!

IT'S SO **ARTSY!**

OH, UH.

WHAT'S YOUR NAME?

UHHH...
OH?!
SO YOU'RE KISHA! I'VE ALWAYS WANTED TO MEET YOU!
SAME!

OH, PLEASE ENTER!
C'MON, KEESH!

WOW...

THIS PLACE
IS TO DIE FOR!

WELCOME, MY LITTLE PIXIES!
THANK YOU FOR YOUR YEARS OF SUPPORTING ME AND MY SHOW!
AND FOR MAKING IT TO MY BIRTHDAY PARTY!
IT'S REALLY HER!!!

LET'S START THIS PARTY WITH AN ICEBREAKER, SHALL WE?
MUSICAL PILLOWS!
LAST ONE STANDING WHEN THE MUSIC ENDS . . .
IS A ROTTEN DEMON!
LET THE PARTY START!
THE RUBY!

LET'S GO! DON'T BE A ROTTEN DEMON!
STOP!
NOW THE OTHER WAY!
STOP!
AW!
LOOKS LIKE YOU'RE A ROTTEN DEMON, SUYIN!
THAT WAS CLOSE. . . .

MEANWHILE . . .
HI, SORRY I'M A LITTLE LATE.
I'M KISHA, HERE FOR THE PARTY.
NICE TRY.
KISHA HAS ALREADY CHECKED IN.
WHAT?
REVERSE AGAIN!
OOF!

STOP!

OH NO . . .

WHAT DO YOU MEAN?! I'M THE REAL KISHA!

UNLESS YOU HAVE PROOF, I'M AFRAID I CAN'T—

HA, SORRY, KISHA.
LOOKS LIKE YOU'RE A . . .
ROTTEN DEMON. . . .
ACTUALLY, I'M STILL ON A PILLOW. . . .
A D-DEMON?!
EXCUSE ME, THERE'S BEEN SOME CONFUSION. . . .

YOU'RE NOT KISHA . . . ?

WHAT THE?!

AHHHHH!!

WAIT, I'M—

WHAT'S GOING ON HERE?

WAIT, MOM! I GOT THIS!
OH NO . . .
HOLD ON! I CAN EXPLAIN!
AH!
EEK!

H-
HELP!
DON'T COME NEAR US!
MOM! I CAN CATCH HER MYSELF!
PLEASE! LET ME DO THIS!

NO, NOUNA!
IT'S TOO DANGEROUS!
YOU CAN HELP BY STAYING OUT OF THIS!
I KNEW I SHOULDN'T HAVE LET YOU RUN YOUR OWN BIRTHDAY PARTY.
AFTER THIS IS OVER . . .
YOU'RE GROUNDED.

I'M SORRY!
I'M SORRY!
YOU'LL PAY FOR THIS, KISHA!!!
FOR RUINING MY BIRTHDAY!

YOU DEMONS ALWAYS RUIN EVERYTHING!
W-WHAT?!
THAT'S . . .
NOT TRUE!
DEMONS AREN'T BAD.

WE'RE GOOD!
HUH?!

W-
WHAT?!
MY
HORNS!

WHOA!

STAY BACK!

DEMON!

SHI NG!

YOU LEAVE ME NO CHOICE.

HA!

N-NOUNA?!
WOOSHHH

YOU'RE DONE FOR!!!

NOUNA, NO! THE VORTEX!
IT WILL SUCK YOU IN!
GOTCHA!

NOUNA!!!
AHHH!!!
MOM!!!
NO!!!
FWPPP

AHHHHHH!

MY HEADBAND!

THIS IS ALL YOUR FAULT!

OUCH!

SPL ASH!

GASP!

AH!

GET AWAY FROM ME!

WHERE ARE WE?!

OH, MIGHTY RUBY, SHINE BRIGHT—
HUH?
I—I'M BACK TO NORMAL?
N—NO!
MY RUBY!
WHERE'S MY RUBY?!
UH . . .
PAT
PAT

I'M SO DEAD.
UHH . . .
IT COULDN'T HAVE GONE TOO FAR!
IT COULD BE SOMEWHERE ON THIS BEACH!

THAT'S NOT HOW IT WORKS!

IF MY RUBY WAS NEAR ME, IT WOULD SHINE WHEN I CALLED FOR IT!

AND THANKS TO YOU, NOW MY MOM WILL NEVER LET ME DO ANYTHING EVER AGAIN.

I HAVE TO FIND IT BEFORE SHE DOES . . . TO PROVE HER WRONG!

MAYBE YOU CAN GET A BETTER VIEW FROM THE SKY?

...
WELL, NOW THAT I DON'T HAVE MY RUBY, I CAN'T FLY!
WAIT, WHAT? BUT YOU'RE A—
OH.
I WAS BORN LIKE THIS, OK?

EVERYTHING YOU'VE SEEN ON TV—IT'S ALL AN ACT, YOU KNOW.

WELL . . . EVEN IF IT WAS ALL AN ACT . . .

I STILL LOVED YOUR SHOW, PRINCESS NOUNA.

HEY, WHERE ARE YOU GOING?!

TO FIND YOUR RUBY! COME ON!

WAIT!
IT'S MINE
TO FIND!
I'M JUST
TRYING TO
HELP YOU!

WAIT UP,
WILL YOU?!

KISHA!

HEY!

OOF!

UGH!
WHOA!

PLUMERIA CITY
AS MANY OF YOU ALREADY KNOW . . .
PRINCESS NOUNA IS MISSING, DUE TO AN INTRUDER.
HER WHEREABOUTS ARE UNKNOWN. AS A RESULT, I WILL BE LEAVING PLUMERIA CITY TO FIND HER.
FOR NOW, YOU WILL ALL BE SAFE UNDER THE PROTECTION OF OUR GUARD.
THIS IS NOT THE FIRST TIME PLUMERIA CITY HAS BEEN GREATLY DISTURBED.
BUT REST ASSURED THAT I WILL MAKE IT THE LAST.
PLEASE REMEMBER TO TAKE CARE AND WATCH OUT FOR ONE ANOTHER.

MEANWHILE . . .

UH . . . I DON'T THINK WE SHOULD GO IN THERE.

IT LOOKS SO DARK AND . . .

SQUISH

SQUISHY?

SHUT
EEK!

WHAT IS THIS PLACE?
I—I CAN'T SEE!
WAIT, YOU CAN'T SEE?
IT'S PITCH-BLACK, WHAT DO YOU EXPECT?
I KNEW I NEVER SHOULD HAVE FOLLOWED A DEMON IN HERE.
I TOLD YOU, DEMONS AREN'T—
HEY!
OH, WAIT! DEMONS CAN SHINE LIGHT WITH OUR EYES AND SEE IN THE DARK!
WHAT?!

C'MON, LOOK! THERE'S A PATH GOING DOWN THERE!
WHOA!
HUH? IT'S GLOWING AGAIN?
MAYBE THIS CAN HELP, TOO?
WE'RE IN . . .
A MOUTH?!

I KNEW IT! THIS WAS A PART OF YOUR DEMON PLAN!
NO! I HAD NO IDEA THIS WAS A MOUTH! I SWEAR!

I WAS JUST TRYING TO HELP.
HUH?!
WHOA . . .
RUMBLE
RUMBLE

WE'RE GONNA DIE!!!

OK, I HAVE ANOTHER PLAN!
ON THE COUNT OF THREE, JUMP!
ONE . . .
TWO . . .
THREE!

NOW JUST HOLD ON UNTIL THE RUMBLING STOPS!
JUMP!
ARE YOU KIDDING ME?!
GOT ANY BETTER IDEAS?!
WHY SHOULD I WHEN NONE OF THIS IS EVEN MY FAULT!

SNIFF
SNIFF
WHAT ARE YOU DOING?
WE HAVE TO STAY ALIVE, YOU KNOW!
IT'S JUST THAT . . .
I NEVER THOUGHT YOU COULD BE SO MEAN!

I'M . . . MEAN?
SNIFF
AHH . . .
AH . . .
AHHH . . .

poot
AH!
I—I DID IT!
WHAT?! YOU CAN FLY?!

GRRR...
WHOA!
WE WERE INSIDE OF THAT THING?!
WHAT?!

WHOOOOAAHHH!
I CAN'T CONTROL MY WINGS!
YOU NEED TO GET FLYING LESSONS AFTER THIS!
OW!
WATCH OUT!

UHHH . . .

POINT IT AT THAT!

ZZZZZZ

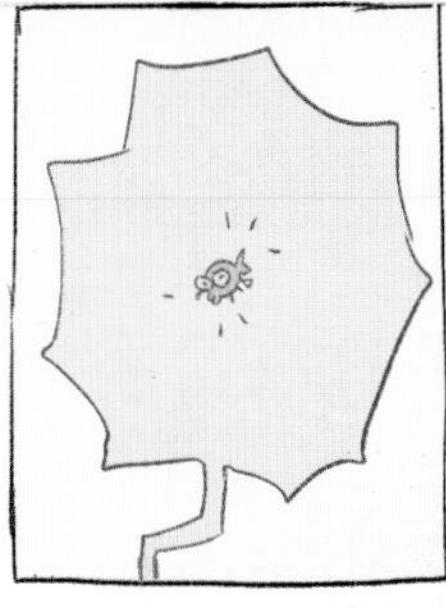

HEY, YOU OK?
HNG . . .

KISHA?

TSSSS...

WHAT JUST HAPPENED?

UH... I DON'T KNOW.

EVERY TIME THIS FANG THING GLOWS, I GET WEIRD POWERS.

HOWEVER YOU DID IT . . .
THANK YOU.

YOU SAVED US.

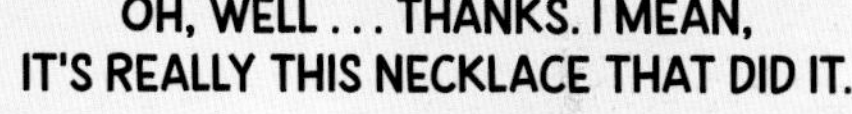
OH, WELL . . . THANKS. I MEAN, IT'S REALLY THIS NECKLACE THAT DID IT.

WHERE'D YOU GET IT FROM?
UH . . .

WELL, I THINK IT'S MY GRANDMA'S.
IT WAS THE ONLY THING I COULD GRAB FROM HER WHEN IT ALL HAPPENED.
WHAT'S "IT"?
UH.
SOMETHING BAD HAPPENED TO THE LAVA BACK IN MOUNT MAGMA. IT JUST . . . STARTED GLOWING, OVERFLOWED, AND DESTROYED EVERYTHING.
THAT'S ACTUALLY WHY I CAME TO PLUMERIA CITY. TO FIND HELP.

I THOUGHT THAT MAYBE YOU AND THE RUBY COULD HELP SAVE IT.
I'M SORRY.
I HAD NO IDEA.
YEAH, WELL.
I'M SORRY, TOO. ABOUT YOUR PARTY. I DIDN'T CRASH IT ON PURPOSE, I SWEAR.
I JUST DIDN'T KNOW WHO ELSE TO GO TO.

BUT MAYBE I CAN FIND SOMEONE ELSE TO HELP.

KISHA! WAIT!

YOU SAVED ME. MAYBE WE CAN HELP EACH OTHER.
WHAT DO YOU SAY TO LOOKING FOR MY RUBY? TOGETHER?

IF WE FIND IT, I'LL SEE WHAT IT CAN DO.

PRINCESS NOUNA . . . WANTS TO HELP ME?
UM . . .

THAT . . . SOUNDS LIKE A PLAN. THANKS, PRINCESS NOUNA.

JUST CALL ME NOUNA, WILL YA?

OH, IN THAT CASE . . . MY REAL NAME IS MEESH.

MEESH? CUTE! YOU'RE NOT AS BAD OF A DEMON AS I THOUGHT YOU WERE!
UHHH, WELL, THANKS!
SO...
WE SHOULD PROBABLY GET OUT OF HERE.
YEAH, WHERE **ARE** WE?

PLUMERIA CITY
BE RIGHT BACK. GONNA TRASH THIS.
HEY, I HAVE BAD NEWS.

WHAT IS IT?
A DEMON GIRL BROKE INTO THE PALACE TODAY.
SHE GOT SUCKED INTO A VORTEX IN AN ATTEMPT TO REMOVE HER . . . BUT THE PRINCESS WAS SUCKED IN WITH HER.
SEEMS LIKE SHE MIGHT'VE COME FROM MOUNT MAGMA. WHEREABOUTS NOW UNKNOWN.
SIGH.

WELL, WHAT'S DONE IS DONE.
THERE'S NO WAY IT CAN BE UNDONE, UNLESS BY THE GUARDIAN.
AND I'M CERTAIN WE'VE GOT THE GUARDIAN.
RIGHT . . . SO, WOULD A REGULAR DEMON JUST HAPPEN TO HAVE THE ABILITY TO COMPLETELY TRANSFORM?

WHAT DO YOU MEAN?
THE DEMON GIRL. SHE TRANSFORMED. SHE HAD POWERS TO FIGHT BACK!
OF COURSE. THIS WOULD HAPPEN.
JUST LET THE QUEEN TAKE CARE OF IT FOR NOW.
THERE'S NO WAY SHE WILL RELEASE A DEMON.

MEANWHILE
SO . . .
ONCE YOU GET THE HANG OF FLYING, YOU GOTTA TEACH ME.

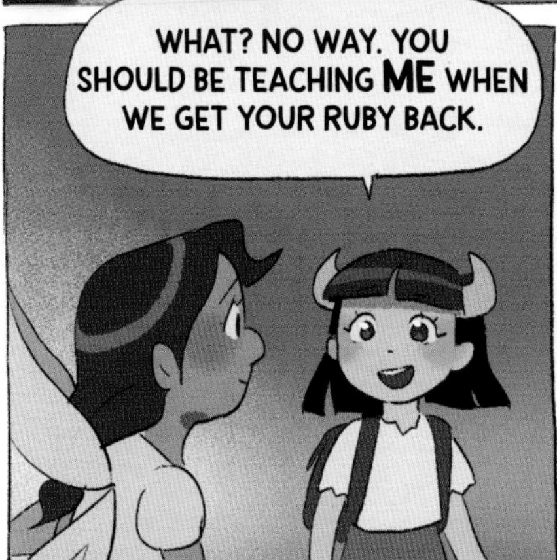
WHAT? NO WAY. YOU SHOULD BE TEACHING ME WHEN WE GET YOUR RUBY BACK.

WELL, I'D LIKE TO LEARN TO FLY WITHOUT IT SOMEDAY.

. . .

NOUNA?

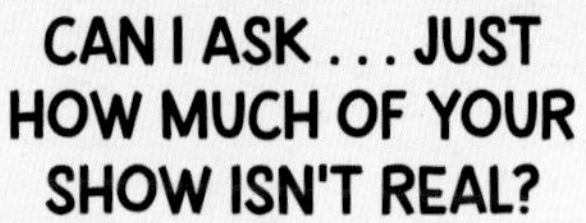
CAN I ASK . . . JUST HOW MUCH OF YOUR SHOW ISN'T REAL?

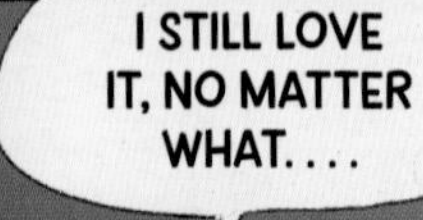

AND I DON'T MEAN THAT IN A BAD WAY!

I STILL LOVE IT, NO MATTER WHAT. . . .

A LOT OF IT.

MOST FAIRY PARENTS TEACH THEIR KIDS HOW TO FLY WHEN THEY'RE BABIES.
BUT WITH MY BROKEN WING, IT MADE IT HARDER FOR MY MOM TO TEACH ME. ESPECIALLY SINCE SHE'S SO BUSY PROTECTING THE FAIRY WORLD.

THE RUBY CONTAINS SOME OF MY MOM'S POWER. THAT'S HOW IT HELPS ME FLY.
BUT WITHOUT IT, I CAN'T.
HONESTLY, I'M SCARED OF OTHER FAIRIES FINDING OUT THE TRUTH.

BUT IF I COULD JUST LEARN TO FLY BY MYSELF, I WOULDN'T HAVE TO WORRY ABOUT THAT.

WELL, I'M PRETTY SURE THAT THE FAIRIES WOULD STILL LOVE YOU EVEN IF YOU CAN'T FLY.

WELL, THANKS.

A CITY?!

MAYBE SOMEONE THERE CAN HELP . . .

IF WE COULD JUST GET DOWN THERE FROM HERE.

HEY, IF I GOT US OUT OF THAT PUFFER, I'M SURE WE CAN—
HUH?!
IT'S GLOWING AGAIN?!
LAST TIME I TOUCHED IT . . .
WHOA!
POOF

HURRY UP! TAKE MY HAND BEFORE I TURN BACK TO NORMAL. I DON'T KNOW HOW LONG THIS LASTS!
ARE YOU SURE? YOUR FLYING WAS KIND OF . . . WONKY.
HOW ELSE ARE WE GOING TO GET DOWN THERE? PLUS, I HAVE TO LEARN SOMETIME, RIGHT?
OK, FINE . . .
IF WE SURVIVE, YOU OWE ME A FLYING LESSON.

YOU SURE
YOU GOT THIS?!
HNG . . .
WHOOAAAAHHH!!!!

IF I COULD JUST GET MY WINGS TO FLAP IN SYNC . . .
C'MON, I DID THIS BEFORE!
MEESH, WE'RE GONNA CRASH INTO THE TREES!
I CAN'T—

OH, HEY, YOU'RE DOING IT!
YEAH! STILL BUMPY! BUT YEAH!
I THINK I'M GONNA THROW UP. . . .

OVER THERE! WE CAN LAND ON THE GRASS.
OOF! WE GOTTA WORK ON THAT. . . .
BUT HEY, YOU DID IT. SO, GOOD JOB, MEESH.
YEAH. RIGHT ON TIME, TOO.

HUH?

C'MON, GET HIM!

THERE ARE CREATURES FROM EVERYWHERE?!
WOW, OTHER CREATURES CAN FLY, TOO!
PRINCESS NOUNA?!

WAIT, CAN I GET A SELFIE WITH YOU?!
MOM, IS THAT PRINCESS NOUNA?
UH, LET'S KEEP WALKING.
UM, HI...

PRINCESS NOUNA?!
SHE'S JUST LEAVING!
S-SORRY! NEXT TIME!

OK, I THINK THE COAST IS CLEAR.

BUT WAIT . . .
I SMELL SOMETHING.
WHAT IS IT?

I THINK IT'S COMING FROM IN THERE!

OOOOHHH!

WELCOME! DO YOU WANT TO ORDER SOMETHING?

MY NAME IS CHAI AND I'LL BE YOUR SERVER!
OH!
IS THAT . . .
BUB-LAVA?
YEAH! WE MAKE OUR OWN!

I'LL TAKE ONE!
I'LL TAKE A CUPCAKE!
SURE THING!

OOOH!
WOW, I THOUGHT THESE COULD ONLY BE MADE IN MOUNT MAGMA.
HERE YA GO!

WHAT'S IN THAT DRINK ANYWAY?
WANNA TRY IT?
UH . . . SURE? I'VE NEVER HAD ANYTHING LIKE THIS BEFORE.
OH, IT'S GOOD!
I KNOW, RIGHT?
DEMONS KNOW HOW TO PACK A PUNCH!

OH, YOU SAID YOU'RE A DEMON? ARE YOU FROM MOUNT MAGMA?
YEAH, WHY?
MY OTHER CUSTOMER IS FROM THERE, TOO.
I'M NOT SURE WHAT'S UP WITH HIM . . . BUT I RAN INTO HIM IN THE FOREST. HE'S BEEN . . . QUIET.
DO YOU THINK YOU MIGHT KNOW HIM?
I MEAN, I CAN ASK . . . ?
EXCUSE ME . . .

WHAT ARE YOU DOING HERE?!

YOU'RE ALIVE?!
I THOUGHT I WAS THE ONLY ONE WHO MADE IT!
SO YOU DO KNOW EACH OTHER!
ONLY ONE WHO MADE WHAT?
I KNEW A LITTLE BUB-LAVA WOULD GET YOU TALKING!

XAVIER . . . DO YOU KNOW WHAT HAPPENED?
I—
I DON'T KNOW.
OH.
PLEASE, TELL ME WHAT I CAN DO TO HELP.

I'VE GOT FOOD AND SHELTER! IT WOULDN'T BE ANY TROUBLE. . . .
FOOD?
THAT NIGHT . . .
SO AFTER MY GRANDMA TURNED TO STONE, I RAN. IT WAS ALL I COULD DO.
I DON'T EVEN KNOW IF EVERYONE IS JUST FROZEN OR DEAD!

WHAT? HOW COME NO ONE HERE IS TALKING ABOUT IT.
YEAH. I'M NOT EVEN SURE IF ANY OTHER DEMONS MADE IT OUT.
WELL, SHOULDN'T WE LET SOMEONE KNOW? LIKE THE NEWS OR SOMETHING?
THERE'S GOTTA BE SOMEONE WHO KNOWS SOMETHING. OR CARES.
WELL . . .

THE TRUTH IS, I'VE NEVER LEFT MOUNT MAGMA BEFORE.
I DIDN'T KNOW WHERE TO GO FOR HELP.
YOU CAME TO THE RIGHT SPOT.
WE CAN FIGURE THIS OUT TOGETHER.
THANKS, CHAI. I HOPE YOU'RE RIGHT.

YEAH, CHAI'S RIGHT.
WE CAN DO THIS.
XAVIER, YOU KNOW MOUNT MAGMA BETTER THAN ANYONE.
AND I WANT TO HELP, TOO!
THAT'S GREAT, BUT . . . DON'T YOU HAVE TO WORK?

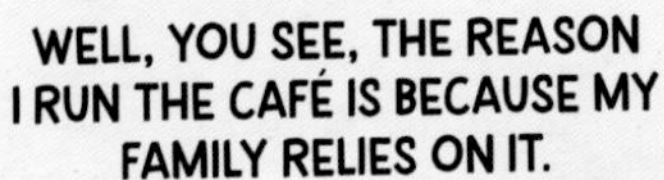
WELL, YOU SEE, THE REASON I RUN THE CAFÉ IS BECAUSE MY FAMILY RELIES ON IT.

WE WERE ALSO FORCED OUT OF OUR HOME.

I'M SO SORRY. HOW DID THAT HAPPEN?
OH NO.

WE'VE NEVER KNOWN FOR SURE. BUT WHAT IF IT WAS THE SAME CAUSE AS MOUNT MAGMA?
WE NEED TO FIND MY RUBY.
I HAVE NO IDEA WHERE IT IS NOW, BUT . . .

IT HAS MAGICAL POWERS THAT MIGHT BE ABLE TO HELP. MEESH THINKS IT COULD SAVE MOUNT MAGMA.
A . . . FAIRY RUBY?

WELL, I'VE NEVER SEEN ONE BEFORE . . .

BUT I HAVE AN IDEA OF WHERE WE CAN LOOK.

AWOOOO!

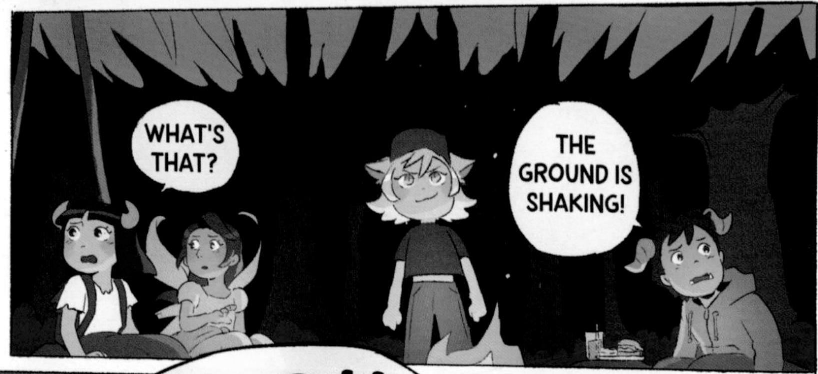
WHAT'S THAT?
THE GROUND IS SHAKING!

AWOOO!!

WOLVES?

SO I MIGHT'VE FORGOTTEN TO MENTION . . . I'M PART WOLF.

WHAT?! THAT'S SO COOL!

C'MON, FOLLOW ME. I'LL SHOW YOU MY IDEA.

BUT HOW?

HOP ON!
DON'T WORRY, THEY'RE MY FAMILY. WE DON'T BITE.

OK . . .

WHOOOAAHHH!

HEY, CHAI, WHERE ARE WE GOING?
TO THE TOP OF THE HILL!
IT ALWAYS HELPS TO GET THE BIG PICTURE!
WOW, THIS IS ACTUALLY PRETTY FUN!
WHEE!

GRANDMA, WE'RE GOING TO SAVE YOU.
HUH?

POOF
YOU CAN DO THAT?!
HEY, SINCE WHEN DO YOU HAVE WINGS?
I'LL RACE YA TO THE TOP!

WHOA!
UH, I'M NOT REALLY THE BEST AT FLY—
AHHH!
YOU SURE YOU GOT THIS?
ONE.
TWO.

HNNNG . . .
MEESH, YOU CAN DO THIS!
REMEMBER THE PUFFER? AND FLYING OFF OF THAT CLIFF?
HEH, THANKS, NOUNA.

HERE, WHY DON'T YOU GIVE IT A SHOT?
WHAT?! I CAN'T! I'M NOT READY FOR THIS!
JUST TRY!
LIKE THIS?
YEAH! JUST LIKE THAT!

JUST COUNT! ONE, TWO, FLAP!
BUT I—
ONE, TWO . . .
FLAP!
SEE, YOU'RE DOING IT!
LIKE IN THAT EPISODE WHERE YOU FLEW OVER A THOUSAND CLOUDS!

EVEN IF YOU SAY IT WAS ALL AN ACT . . .

TO ME . . .

YOU WERE ALWAYS REAL!

OH MY LAVA . . .

AH, MY SCRUNCHIE!
DON'T WORRY!
YOU DON'T HAVE TO BE PERFECT.
WOW, THAT'S AMAZING.

WE CAN BE BAD AT THIS!
TOGETHER!
AHA!
AWOOOOOOOO!

WELL, HERE WE ARE.
THIS IS WHERE WE MOVED AFTER WE LOST OUR HOME.
WOW . . . I NEVER KNEW THE WORLD WAS SO BIG.
YEP. RIGHT NOW WE'RE IN PONDEROSA.
THE PLACE WHERE ALL KINDS OF CREATURES LIVE TOGETHER!

SOMETIMES YOU CAN SEE PLUMERIA CITY UP THERE.

AND, UH . . . MOUNT MAGMA. . . .

SORRY, IT'S FOGGIER THAN USUAL TODAY.

WELL, I WANTED TO SHOW YOU THE VIEW. TO SEE IF IT SPARKED ANY IDEAS.

THIS IS BEAUTIFUL, BUT . . .

I DON'T HAVE ANY IDEAS.

WAIT—

THAT BUILDING— IT LOOKS FAMILIAR!

WASN'T IT IN THE BACKGROUND OF AN EPISODE OF YOUR SHOW? THE ONE WITH THE LOST TREASURE?

OH, THAT? IT'S THE CITY'S MUSEUM.

UH . . .

UH, MAYBE? I'VE NEVER ACTUALLY BEEN THERE BEFORE.

THAT PLACE HAS . . . LOTS OF OLD STUFF.

YOU KNOW, ARTIFACTS, FOSSILS . . .

LIKE, FROM DIFFERENT CREATURES?

THEN WE HAVE TO GO.

WHAT?

YOUR RUBY DIDN'T LAND ON THE BEACH WITH US, NOUNA.

THE VORTEX TOOK IT SOMEWHERE ELSE!

SO WHAT? YOU THINK SOMEONE FOUND IT AND PUT IT IN A MUSEUM? EVEN IF THEY DID, WHAT ARE WE GONNA DO?

GET IT BACK.

NO MATTER WHAT IT TAKES. STEALING MIGHT BE BAD . . .
BUT LOSING MOUNT MAGMA FOREVER IS WORSE.

AND EVEN IF IT'S NOT THERE, MUSEUMS HAVE A LOT OF HISTORY, RIGHT? WE MIGHT FIND SOMETHING ELSE THAT COULD HELP US.

...

...
...

FINE. LET'S DO IT.

IF IT'S THERE, WE'RE STEALING FOR THE GREATER GOOD, RIGHT?

YEAH! AND HONESTLY, MY FAMILY AND I HAVE NOTHING LEFT TO LOSE AT THIS POINT. I'M IN.

XAVIER?
I NEVER THOUGHT I'D SEE THE DAY . . .
YOU'D BE WILLING TO STEAL.
SO . . . WE'RE ALL ON BOARD?
YEP!

IF WE'RE GOING TO DO THIS . . .
WE'LL NEED AN ESCAPE ROUTE.
WE'RE A TEAM. IF ONE PERSON GETS CAUGHT, WE ALL GET CAUGHT.
AND I'M SURE THEY HAVE GUARDS.
AND ALARMS.
WELL, THE MUSEUM'S CENTER DOESN'T LOOK LIKE IT HAS A ROOF—SO IT MUST BE A COURTYARD.

SO IF WE FIND THE RUBY, WE'LL MEET THERE, WHERE NOUNA CAN FLY US OUT.
BUT—
I'M NOT EVEN GOOD AT IT YET! WHAT IF—
YOUR RUBY, NOUNA!
IF YOU HAVE IT, YOU CAN FLY! YOU CAN SAVE US ALL.
YEAH, AND XAVIER AND I CAN, UH, CREATE SOME DISTRACTIONS.

OK,
SO . . .
WE HAVE
A PLAN?

YEP!
WELL . . .

IF WE'RE
GOING TO FIND
THIS RUBY . . .

WE SHOULD PROBABLY
GET ENOUGH SLEEP TO
BRING OUR A-GAME.

I HOPE YOU DON'T MIND CAMPING . . . WE'RE STILL LOOKING FOR A NEW PLACE TO LIVE.

BUT I ACTUALLY LIKE IT HERE NOW.

I GUESS I COULD GET USED TO THIS!
I DON'T KNOW, IT'S STILL KIND OF WEIRD TO ME TO SLEEP WHILE IT'S DARK OUT.
YEAH.
WELL . . .
LET'S HOPE AFTER TOMORROW WE CAN GO HOME.

AT THE MUSEUM . . .

HERE YOU GO.
FOUR TICKETS.

THANKS, SIR!

LET'S START OVER THERE?

SORRY . . . I GOT DISTRACTED.

LET'S SEE . . .

HEY, ISN'T THAT THE RUBY IN THAT PAINTING?

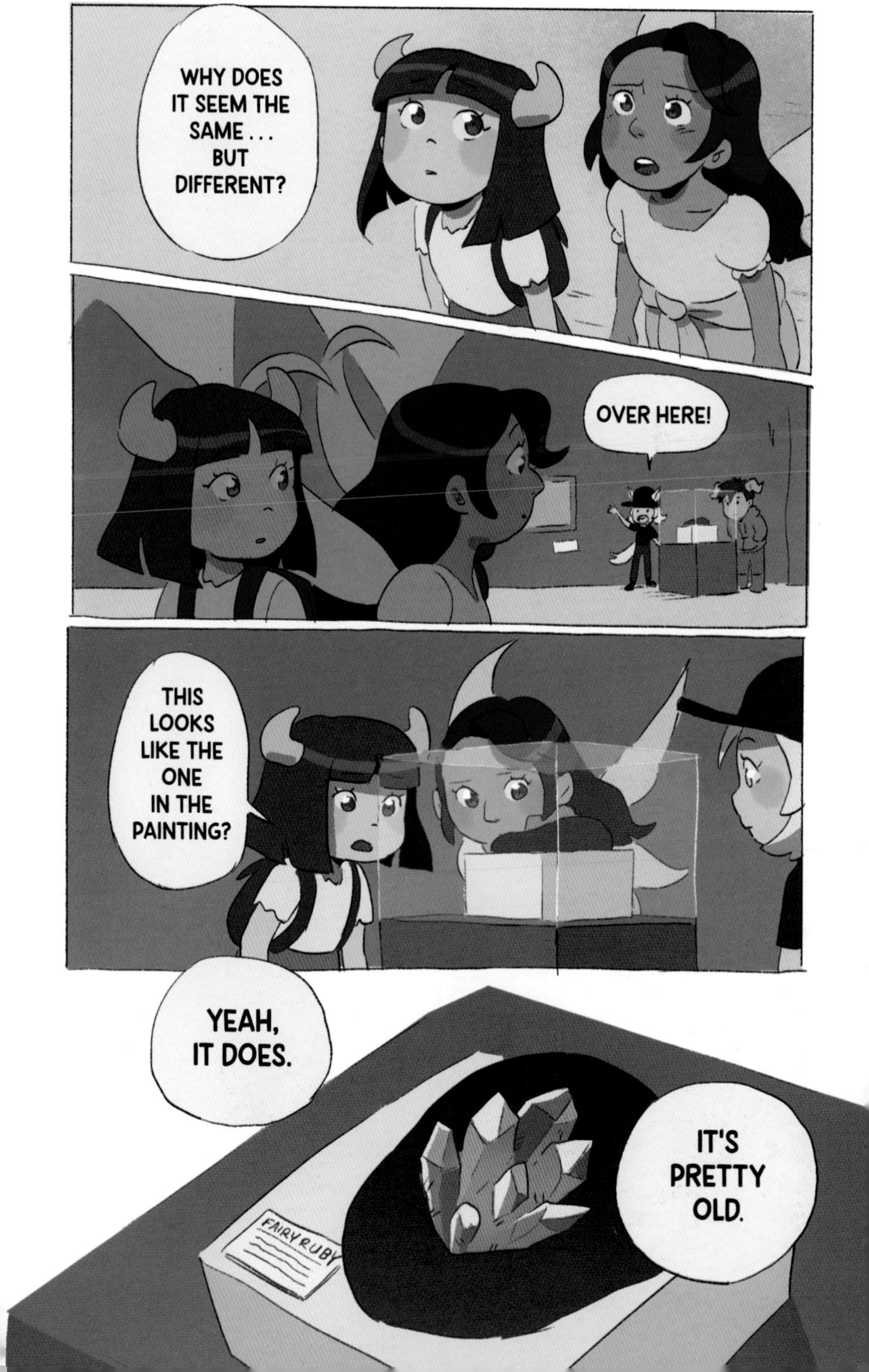

WHY DOES IT SEEM THE SAME . . . BUT DIFFERENT?

OVER HERE!

THIS LOOKS LIKE THE ONE IN THE PAINTING?

YEAH, IT DOES.
IT'S PRETTY OLD.
FAIRY RUBY

IS THERE A CHANCE THIS COULD WORK THE SAME WAY?
NO. IT DOESN'T HAVE ANY POWER IN IT. I CAN TELL.
WELL, IT FEELS LIKE WE'RE GETTING CLOSER. RIGHT?

LET'S LOOK OVER THIS WAY.
WHY ARE WE WALKING SO FAST?
MEESH?

WE'RE MISSING ALL THESE ROOMS.
CAN YOU JUST . . .
SLOW DOWN?
!
HUH?
OH.
I GUESS YOU WERE ONTO SOMETHING.

WHO WOULD HAVE THOUGHT THERE'D BE A HALL DEDICATED TO ROCKS AND CRYSTALS?
WELL, THE MUSEUM IS LITERALLY MADE OF ROCK. . . .

OOH, POINTY.
WOW . . .

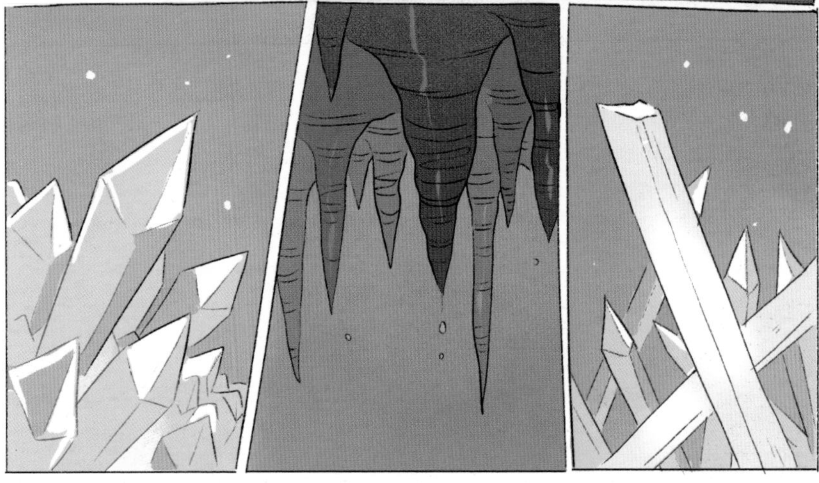

HEY, LOOK! THERE ARE RUBIES ALL OVER THIS PROJECTION.
BUT WHY DO SO MANY OF THE FAIRIES LOOK . . . SCARED?

AND THERE ARE DEMONS, TOO . . . BUT WHAT ARE THEY DOING?
I MEAN, YOU MUST HAVE LEARNED ABOUT THIS IN SCHOOL, RIGHT?

IS THAT
REALLY
WHAT . . .
HAPPENED?

MEESH, OVER HERE!

I'M PRETTY SURE
THAT'S IT.

NO WAY . . .

GUARDS. OF COURSE.

YEAH, THIS MIGHT BE A BIT TRICKY.
WHAT DO WE DO NOW?

THIS IS WHERE BEING PART WOLF COMES IN HANDY.

I'LL GET THE FIRST GUARD. IF THE OTHER ONE STAYS AROUND . . .

XAVIER, YOU KNOW WHAT TO DO.

psssss...

HUH?

PETS ARE NOT ALLOWED ON THIS PROPERTY!
HEY!

GET BACK HERE!
A PET?!

HA!
HA!
PFT!
HA!

OK, NOW LET'S FOCUS
ON THE OTHER GUARD.
SIGNAL ME WHEN YOU'RE CLOSE TO THE RUBY, AND I'LL BLOW ENOUGH SMOKE TO HIDE YOU. THEN BREAK THE GLASS, GRAB IT, AND RUN.
OK, XAVIER. THANKS.
I GUESS I'LL FINALLY GET TO SEE YOU BREATHE FIRE THEN, HUH?

HA, YEAH.
OK, SO AFTER XAVIER SMOKES IT OUT . . .
I CAN GUIDE US WITH MY VISION.
SOUNDS GOOD!
PHEW.
LET'S DO THIS.

SO, YOU REALLY THINK FIRE CAN BREAK THIS THING?
UH . . .
WOW, IT'S A REAL SHAME THAT THE FAIRIES DID THAT.
YEAH, WITH THAT OTHER CRYSTAL.
TO THE DEMONS?
MAYBE YOUR HORNS ARE SHARP ENOUGH?

THEY STOLE THE LAVA SOURCE FROM THE DEMONS TO CREATE THAT OTHER RUBY . . .
AND THEN USED IT TO THREATEN THEM BECAUSE THE FAIRIES NEEDED MORE LAVA. WHAT A CYCLE.
YEAH, IT WAS HUNDREDS OF YEARS AGO, BUT STILL. . . .
SO WHICH DO YOU THINK IS BETTER? HORNS OR FIRE?
WHAT?

NOUNA . . . YOU'RE SURE THAT THE FAIRIES HAD NOTHING TO DO WITH WHAT HAPPENED IN MOUNT MAGMA, RIGHT?
WHAT? WHY WOULD YOU EVEN ASK THAT?
ALL THOSE VIDEOS PLAYING ON THE PROJECTOR!
IS THAT WHY FAIRIES AND DEMONS ARE SO DIVIDED?
THOSE ARE, LIKE, FROM HISTORY!
WHAT ARE YOU ACCUSING ME OF, MEESH?

MEESH . . .
EVEN WHEN I FIRST GOT TO PLUMERIA CITY, YOU ALL TREATED ME LIKE . . .
WHY ARE YOU BRINGING THIS UP NOW? WE NEED TO STICK TO THE PLAN!
LIKE I WAS A MONSTER!
NO!
OW!

GASP!
FIRE! EMERGENCY IN THE CRYSTAL HALL!
FIRE?!
HUH? I GUESS THAT'S THE SIGNAL.

ATTENTION, EVERYONE!
WE MUST EVACUATE!

HEY!

AHHH!

THERE'S STILL A CHANCE. . . .
MAYBE I CAN . . .
CRASH
WAIT, MEESH!
GOT IT!

TO THE COURTYARD! SO WE CAN FLY OUT!
HUH?
WHY?!
C'MON! TRANSFORM ME!
HURRY UP AND FLY!
MEESH . . .
HEY, WHAT'S HAPPENING?

WHY AREN'T YOU WORKING?!
C'MON! WE HAVE TO SAVE MOUNT—
STOP!
GIVE ME BACK MY RUBY!
I THOUGHT WE WERE DOING THIS TOGETHER!

AND I THOUGHT I COULD TRUST YOU!
WHAT?!
I KEPT MY PROMISE!
YOU'RE THE ONE WHO LIED.

NOUNA, I DIDN'T . . .

AH!

MOM?
LOOK! IT'S THE FAIRY QUEEN!
NO WAY!
WAIT, NO!
I'LL TAKE IT FROM HERE!

SHE SAVED US?
WHOA . . .
WOW!
I DON'T THINK THIS WAS PART OF THE PLAN.
MEESH?
NOUNA?

EVERYONE, EVACUATE!
THE MUSEUM WILL BE SHUTTING ITS DOORS EARLY DUE TO THIS EMERGENCY!

PLUMERIA CITY
WELL, NOUNA . . .
WOULD YOU CARE TO EXPLAIN EVERYTHING?
ME? EXPLAIN? WHAT ABOUT YOU? HOW DID YOU EVEN KNOW WHERE TO FIND ME?

BACK WHEN THE VORTEX GOT YOU . . .

THE RUBY NEVER EXITED THE PALACE. IT WAS LEFT BEHIND.

I KNEW IT WOULD BE IMPOSSIBLE TO FIND YOU SINCE VORTEXES RELEASE IN UNPREDICTABLE LOCATIONS. YOU COULD'VE BEEN ANYWHERE.

BUT I KNEW YOU NEEDED THE RUBY.

I SET OUT TO FIND ANOTHER PLACE WHERE FAIRY RUBIES AND CRYSTALS EXIST.
SO I LEFT IT AT THE MUSEUM, KNOWING THERE WAS A CHANCE YOU MIGHT GO SEARCHING FOR IT.
MAKE SURE YOU'RE RECORDING AT ALL TIMES. I'LL RETURN IF I SEE MY DAUGHTER.
YES, MA'AM.

I KNEW YOU'D AVOID COMING HOME BEFORE FINDING THE RUBY.
AND THERE YOU WERE.

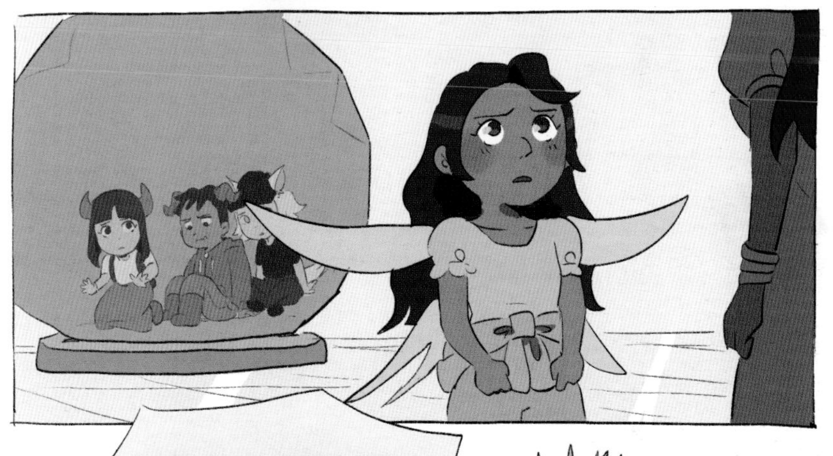

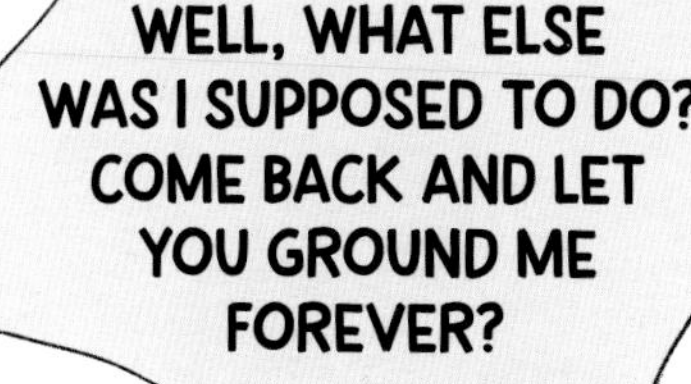
WELL, WHAT ELSE WAS I SUPPOSED TO DO? COME BACK AND LET YOU GROUND ME FOREVER?

AND LOOK WHAT HAPPENED WHEN YOU STAYED OUT THERE!
YOU TRUSTED AN INTRUDER, ONLY TO BE BETRAYED BY YOUR OWN "FRIEND"!
YOU THINK THESE CREATURES REALLY CARE ABOUT YOU?
NOUNA, TELL HER!

SIGH.

ENOUGH. WHERE ARE YOUR PARENTS? THEY NEED TO BE HELD ACCOUNTABLE FOR THIS. FOR YOU TRYING TO STEAL A FAIRY ARTIFACT!

WELL, IF IT WEREN'T FOR **YOU** FAIRIES . . .

MY GRANDMA WOULD BE HERE. BUT SHE ISN'T. BECAUSE **YOU** POISONED MOUNT MAGMA!

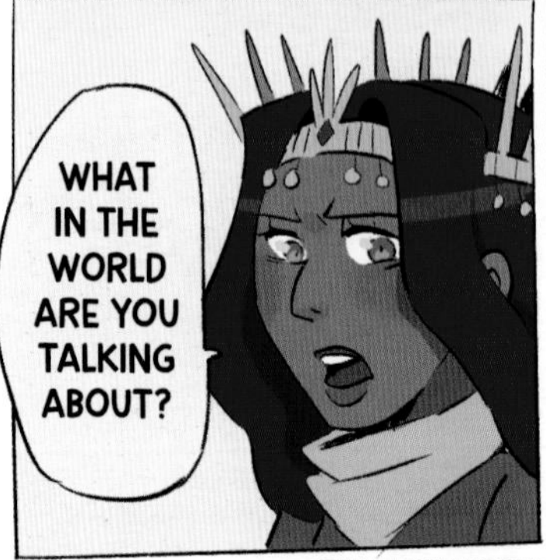
WHAT IN THE WORLD ARE YOU TALKING ABOUT?

THE GREEN GLOW? IN THE LAVA? TURNING EVERYONE INTO STONE?

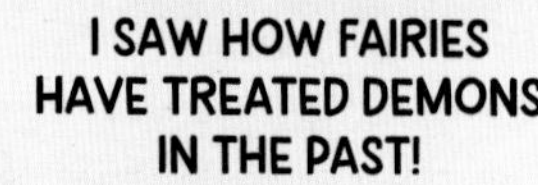
I SAW HOW FAIRIES HAVE TREATED DEMONS IN THE PAST!

HOW DARE YOU ACCUSE—

YOU THREATENED US SO WE'D GIVE YOU **OUR** LAVA SO YOU COULD CREATE MORE RUBIES. AND NOW YOU'VE RETURNED TO POISON OUR ENTIRE CITY.
MEESH!
NONSENSE.

ARE YOU AWARE OF HOW BOLD YOUR ACCUSATIONS ARE?
BUT IT'S ALL THE TRUTH.
NOUNA, YOU MUST SEE HOW BEFRIENDING THESE CREATURES TARNISHES PLUMERIA CITY'S REPUTATION.
I'M AFRAID THAT AFTER THIS . . .

I KNOW WHAT HAPPENED, OK?!

I KNOW WHO POISONED MOUNT MAGMA.
AND WHY SHOULD I BELIEVE ANYTHING YOU HAVE TO SAY?
I CAN SHOW YOU WHERE IT HAPPENED. JUST—PLEASE—LISTEN TO ME.
XAVIER . . .
WHY DIDN'T YOU TELL US SOONER?

I JUST . . .

DIDN'T WANT ANYONE TO BLAME ME INSTEAD.

SHE'S A THIEF, NOUNA, WHO TRIED TO STEAL YOUR RUBY AND LEAVE YOU POWERLESS FOREVER.
YOU WANT US TO HELP THEM AFTER EVERYTHING SHE SAID ABOUT US?
!
THAT'S NOT WHAT HAPPENED!
AND WITHOUT MEESH, I NEVER WOULD HAVE LEARNED TO FLY ON MY OWN.
NOUNA?!

MEESH CAME HERE ON MY BIRTHDAY LOOKING FOR **HELP**.

AND WE TREATED HER LIKE SHE WAS A MONSTER.

ALL SHE WANTED TO DO WAS SAVE HER HOME.

NOUNA . . .

HOW CAN YOU BLAME HER FOR THINKING FAIRIES WERE BEHIND IT?

ESPECIALLY WHEN FAIRIES HAVE ALL THE WRONG IDEAS ABOUT WHAT DEMONS ARE LIKE!
I'M SORRY, MEESH.
WELL, MAYBE WE CAN SHOW THE FAIRIES—AND THE DEMONS—WHAT WE'RE REALLY LIKE BY GIVING EACH OTHER A CHANCE.
SEE, MOM?

WE CAN MAKE THINGS RIGHT. WE CAN SAVE MOUNT MAGMA. TOGETHER!

WELL . . . OK. I'M TRUSTING YOU, NOUNA. THIS IS YOUR LAST CHANCE.

WE'LL HAVE TO RETURN TO THE SOURCE. IT'S THE ONLY WAY TO FIGURE OUT IF WE **CAN** HELP.

WE'LL LEAVE NOW.

SO . . . YOU'RE SAYING YOU'LL TRY?

nod

WOOOSHH
LET'S GO.
THANK YOU.

FWSSHHH
WE'RE FLYING?!
WHOA!
HEHE!
NOUNA AND MEESH, YOU CAN FLY ON YOUR OWN, YES?
THE SPELL GRANTS TEMPORARY FLYING POWERS. IT WILL WEAR OFF AS SOON AS WE GET TO MOUNT MAGMA.

YOU BET!
OK THEN. ONWARD.
CAREFUL NOW.
MEESH, WHERE ARE YOUR WINGS?
WOOHOO! NOW I'M A PART OF THE FLYING CLUB!

MY NECKLACE ISN'T WORKING . . . AND I DON'T KNOW WHY.

WELL, IN THAT CASE . . .

YOU KNOW THE DRILL.

THANKS, NOUNA.

ALMOST THERE NOW . . .

XAVIER,
Y-YOU
KNOW THE
WAY, RIGHT?

OVER HERE!

START BY TELLING US WHAT HAPPENED.

OW!

WELL . . . MAYBE . . .

I . . . I KEPT GETTING BAD SCORES IN LAVA-MOLDING CLASS.
I STUDIED SO HARD, BUT FOR SOME REASON, I COULD NEVER GET IT RIGHT.
WHAT'S THIS C ABOUT, XAVIER?
I'LL DO BETTER, MOM. I PROMISE.
YOU CAN. AND YOU WILL.
I STARTED PRACTICING ON MY OWN AT A NEARBY LAKE.

WOW!
A FISH!
I WISH I COULD DO THAT.
HOW DID YOU DO IT?!
OH, YOU'RE NEW HERE.

BY THE LOOKS OF YOUR UNIFORM, YOU MUST BE FROM MOUNT MAGMA MIDDLE SCHOOL, RIGHT?

YEAH. I'M PRACTICING FOR MY NEXT LAVA-MOLDING TEST . . .

BUT I ALWAYS BURN MYSELF.
WELL, I CAN SHOW YOU HOW TO DO IT—WITHOUT EVEN TOUCHING THE LAVA.

MEET ME BACK HERE TOMORROW.

YOU'LL DEFINITELY BLOW YOUR CLASS AWAY WITH THIS ONE.

SO THE NEXT DAY, I MET UP WITH HER BACK AT THIS VERY SPOT.
HEY THERE! YOU READY?
I MAKE THIS OINTMENT FOR LAVA MOLDING.
WHEN YOU DIP YOUR HANDS IN . . .
IT SHOULD BE PAINLESS.
AND THERE YOU GO! IT MAKES THE LAVA FLOAT. ALMOST LIKE MAGNETS.
THEN YOU CAN START MOLDING IT WITHOUT LAYING A FINGER ON IT.

TA-DA!

NO WAY!

WANNA GIVE IT A GO?

RUB YOUR HANDS TOGETHER.

DON'T BE AFRAID! IT WON'T BURN.

WHOA! I'M DOING IT!
WOW.
THANK YOU SO MUCH.
SURE THING.
HERE. I'LL GIVE YOU A FRESH NEW ONE.
CONSIDER IT A GIFT FROM ME.
AND GOOD LUCK ON YOUR NEXT EXAM.

ARE YOU SERIOUS?!
OF COURSE! YOU KIDS NEED SAFER WAYS TO LEARN IN SCHOOL.

THEN, AFTER THAT INCIDENT WE HAD AT SCHOOL . . .
NO!

WE NEED TO GET HELP!

I REALIZED THE VIAL MIGHT HAVE FALLEN OUT OF MY POCKET WHILE WE WERE ARGUING.

WAIT, I THINK I MIGHT HAVE LOST SOMETHING.
I MUST HAVE DROPPED IT WHEN SHE . . .
YOU KNOW WHAT? FORGET IT. LET'S KEEP GOING.
IF SHE'S HURT, WE'RE DEAD.
WAIT.

IS THAT WHAT YOU DROPPED?
JEEZ, IT'S SO SMALL. WHAT IS IT?
OH, YEAH, UH . . .
C'MON, LET'S GO.

HUH?

YOUR FINGER . . .

WHAT?

IT'S CHANGING. . . .
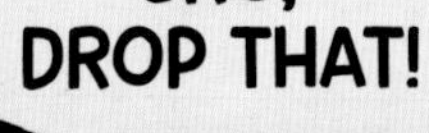
BRO, DROP THAT!

WHAT'S IN THAT?
SOME EXPIRED LOTION?

SPLASH

POOSH

HUH?
IT MADE THE LAVA EXPLODE?

GUYS . . .
YOUR
ARMS.
YOUR
FACES.

OUR
WHAT?

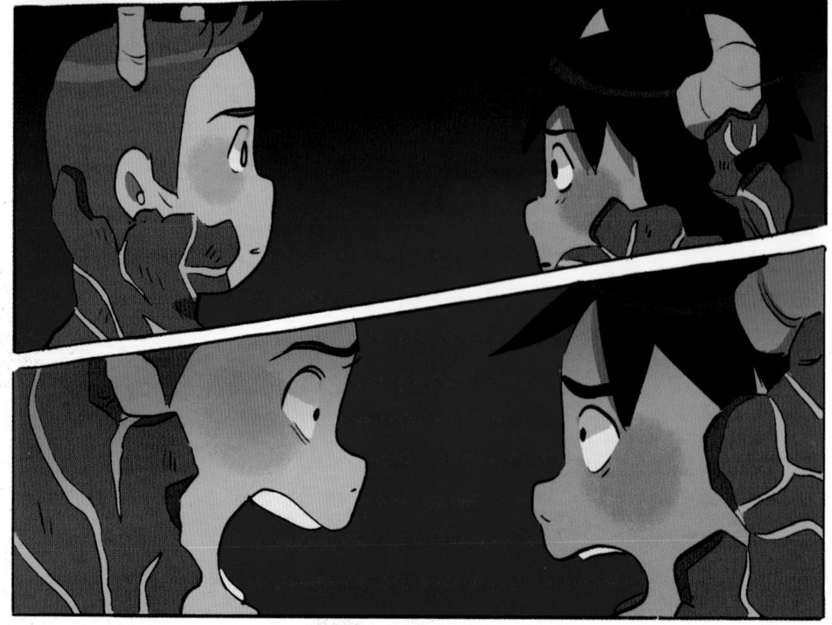

AHHHHH!

AND THAT'S WHEN . . .

I REALIZED I'D BEEN LIED TO.

NO.
THIS CAN'T BE.

I—
I'M SO SORRY.

MOM!
GASP!

XAVIER . . . THERE'S SOMETHING WRONG WITH THE LAVA.

SO I RAN AWAY. AS FAR AS I COULD GET FROM MOUNT MAGMA.

ALL MY FAULT. . . .
AH!
OOF . . .
UGH . . .

HMM?
sniff
sniff

HEY!
HEY! YOU OK?

JEEZ, YOU'RE FREEZING!

LET'S GET YOU SOMEWHERE SAFE.

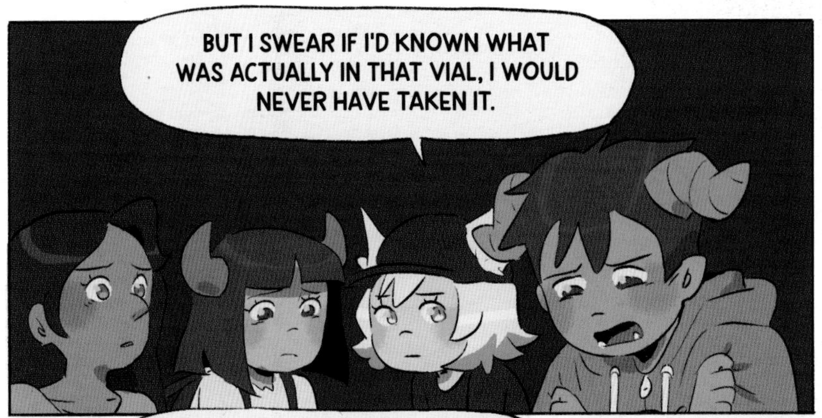
BUT I SWEAR IF I'D KNOWN WHAT WAS ACTUALLY IN THAT VIAL, I WOULD NEVER HAVE TAKEN IT.

SO, THIS ALL HAPPENED BECAUSE OF A RANDOM STRANGER?

I MEAN . . . YEAH.

A VIAL FILLED WITH POISON . . .
IF YOU'RE TELLING THE TRUTH, SOMEONE POWERFUL IS BEHIND THIS.

AND . . . I'M AFRAID THE DAMAGE IS FAR GREATER THAN WHAT THE RUBY AND EVEN MY OWN POWERS ARE CAPABLE OF.
WE HAVE TO TRY!
THE RUBY, PLEASE!
WELL . . .

OH, MIGHTY RUBY, SHINE BRIGHT . . .
DESTROY THIS EVIL . . .
WITH ALL YOUR LIGHT!

...
HMM...
UH...
SORRY, MEESH...
I DON'T THINK...
IT'S GOING TO...

I JUST CAN'T BELIEVE . . .
IT TOOK ME THIS LONG TO REALIZE . . .
THAT I DO LOVE BEING A DEMON.

MEESH! YOUR NECKLACE!
WAIT . . .
THAT'S IT!
YES!

THIS IS WHAT
THE NECKLACE
WAS FOR!

HUH?
WHY DIDN'T IT WORK?
UH...
WHY IS THIS HAPPENING?!

MEESH!

I DON'T THINK IT'S . . .

HNG!

SO . . .
THERE'S NOTHING WE CAN DO?

IF YOU WANT, WE CAN FIND A NEW HOME TOGETHER.
YES.
WE CAN ARRANGE A PLACE FOR YOU TO STAY IN PLUMERIA CITY, TOO.
YOU'LL BE TAKEN CARE OF WHILE WE KEEP TRYING.

THERE HAS TO BE ANOTHER WAY. WE CAN TRY AGAIN, TOGETHER!
THANK YOU, EVERYONE.
IT'S GOING TO BE OK.
OH!
SORRY ABOUT THAT. . . .

LET ME JUST UNTANGLE THESE.
WAIT, NOUNA. . . .
LOOK! DO YOU SEE WHAT I SEE?
WHAT?
YOUR RUBY AN MY FANG FIT PERFECTL TOGETHE

THEY'RE . . .
THEY'RE
GLOWING.

I THINK IT'S . . .
WORKING!

WOW!
OH MY . . .

CRK
CRACK
HUH?
WHAT HAPPENED?

WE'RE . . .
WE'RE
BACK!
OW, MY HEAD . . .
WE'RE ALIVE!

NOUNA, LOOK!
EVERYTHING IS REPAIRING ITSELF!
THIS IS THE MOUNT MAGMA I KNOW!

THAT MEANS . . .
FOLLOW ME!

GRANDMA . . . ?
poof

GRANDMA!

MEESH, YOU'RE OK!
WHAT HAPPENED?

I GOT HELP
FROM PLUMERIA CITY!

I MET PRINCESS NOUNA
AND THE FAIRY QUEEN!

WELL, THANK YOU. BUT MEESH IS THE HERO BEHIND ALL OF THIS, NOT ME.

I COULDN'T HAVE DONE ANY OF IT WITHOUT THIS FANG NECKLACE, THOUGH.

OH.
IT SEEMS LIKE YOU BEAT ME TO THE PUNCH. . . .

I PROBABLY SHOULD'VE TOLD YOU SOONER. . . .

I . . . WAS THE GUARDIAN
OF MOUNT MAGMA.

WAIT, WAIT—
WHAT?! SO
THIS FANG . . .
HAS GUARDIAN
POWERS?!
WELL,
YES,
BUT . . .

I RETIRED
FROM IT
AFTER YOUR
MOM CAME
INTO THE
PICTURE.
SO I
CHANNELED
MY POWER
INTO THIS FANG
TO EVENTUALLY
PASS ON TO YOUR
MOTHER . . .
AND NOW
TO YOU.

BUT
HOW CAN
I PROTECT
MOUNT
MAGMA?!
I'M JUST
A KID!

MEESH, YOU DON'T HAVE TO BE A CERTAIN AGE . . .
TO BE A HERO.
PLUS, YOU HAVE US NOW!
YEAH! TOGETHER WE'RE, LIKE, 50!
WELL, WE HAVE TO FIND THE STRANGER. THE ONE WHO DID THIS.
YOU KNOW WHO DID THIS?!

YES. SHE TRICKED ME AND PLANTED THE POISON. SHE KNEW WHAT WOULD HAPPEN.

OH MY.

THE CITY OF PLUMERIA WILL HELP YOU GET TO THE BOTTOM OF THIS.

I'M NOT THE GUARDIAN ANYMORE . . .

AND WE CAN'T DO IT ALONE.

AND WHY SHOULD **WE** TRUST **YOU**?

WE'LL NEVER FORGET WHAT HAPPENED IN THE PAST.

YOU WON'T BE ALONE THIS TIME.

YEAH!

WE DON'T HAVE TO FORGET THE PAST! BUT RIGHT NOW WE NEED HELP.
WE HAVE TO TRUST THEM.

WE HAVE TO AT LEAST TRY.

TOGETHER.

RIGHT!

ALL OF US.

YEAH!

LOOK AT US. DEMONS AND FAIRIES, WORKING TOGETHER.
HOPEFULLY . . .
THIS IS THE START OF A NEW CHAPTER IN OUR HISTORY.
XAVIER!
MY BABY!
MOM?!

I'M SO GLAD YOU'RE OK!
MY BRAVE BOY.
I'M PROUD OF YOU, MEESH.
THANKS, GRANDMA.

EVA.
UPDATE: THE DEMON GIRL, SHE . . . SHE RESTORED MOUNT MAGMA.
SO THAT PROVES IT. WE WERE WRONG ABOUT THE GUARDIAN ALL ALONG.
AND YOU KNOW HOW MUCH I **HATE** BEING WRONG.

BUT AFTER THIS . . .
SHE'LL WISH SHE NEVER REVEALED HERSELF.